MIGHTY ALICE

Goes Round and Round

Other Cul de Sac Books
by Richard Thompson

Cul de Sac: This Exit

Children at Play

Cul de Sac Golden Treasury

Shapes and Colors

The Mighty Alice

A *Cul de Sac* book

Richard Thompson

Andrews McMeel Publishing, LLC
Kansas City • Sydney • London

Cul de Sac is distributed internationally by Universal Uclick.

Andrews McMeel Publishing, LLC
an Andrews McMeel Universal company
1130 Walnut Street, Kansas City, Missouri 64106

www.andrewsmcmeel.com

13 14 15 16 17 SHO 10 9 8 7 6 5 4 3 2 1

ISBN: 978-1-4494-3721-3

Library of Congress Control Number: 2012954162

Made by:
Shanghai Offset Printing Products LTD
Address and place of production:
No. 1320, Xinwei, Liguang Community,
Guanlan Subdistrict, Bao'an District, Shenzhen,
Guangdong Province, China 518110
1st printing – 4/22/13

My name is Alice Otterloop, and I'm 4 years old.
I live in Cul de Sac, a suburban community ringed by a mighty wall and girded by a moat of stagnant traffic. Its placid exterior hides mysteries to chill the blood!
CUL DE SAC
R. Thompson

Yonder stands the Haunted Gazebo, where no one ever dares set foot. Yet, on Midsummer's Eve, it's suffused with a spectral light, and the murmured prayers of ghostly Druid priests can be heard!
CUL DE SAC
Or the Uncanny Old Lady, a throwback to a time before Cul de Sac! From her kitsch-filled yard she beckons, seeking to turn the unwary into small yappy dogs with her dire magic!
What'd she say?
ALICE! Stop being silly and come talk to your Grandma!

This is the Blisshaven Academy, A Preschool, the scene of my daily toil.

That's the official crest. It shows a preschooler rampant on a field of green, clutching a crayon in each hand. Beneath is a banner with the school motto, "A Little Learning."
THE BLISSHAVEN ACADEMY
A LITTLE LEARNING
A PRESCHOOL

How do you know all this stuff?
My Mom read the school brochure to me.
And my brother Petey went here.

Petey did?
You can still see the scratches his fingernails made on the sidewalk when he was dragged into school one memorable Monday.
So much for my theory about the giant chicken.
R. thompson

Good morning, Alice. It's your turn to make the morning announcements.
I know, Miss Bliss!

I'd like to cover some issues affecting me, like how few marsh-mallows were in my cereal at breakfast, and that dumb radio station my Mom listens to in the van.

No, we just need to hear the weather, how the class avocado plant is doing, and what the Shape of the Day is. Okay?

I think my lack of marshmallows is more interesting than that avocado plant.
Who am I to argue?

Good morning, class, this is Alice Otterloop with the announcements.
It will be mostly sunny today.
Our avocado plant, "Mr. Avocado Plant," is doing well.

The Triangle is the Shape of the Day.
AND MY CEREAL AT BREAKFAST HAD ONLY THREE MARSHMALLOWS AND THEY WERE ALL GREEN!
THANK YOU ALICE. CLASS, IT'S STORY TIME.
ADVANCED MOTHER GOOSE

Humpty Dumpty
Used caution & care,
Instead of a wall
He sat on a chair!
STORY TIME
See?

That was it?
Where's the drama? Where's the conflict?
How's this? Humpty Dumpty Started to crack, 'Cause Humpty Dumpty Sat on a tack.
That's good! Did you write that?

Miss Bliss, what kind of egg was Humpty Dumpty?
Well, it doesn't say-
A duck egg!
A GOOSE EGG!
I'll bet he was the egg of that chicken who crossed the road!

'Cause they're both thrill-seekers with dangerous hobbies.
Good point.
Whew! I think I've learned enough for today. Miss Bliss, can I go home?

The books at this school are falling apart. Look at all the loose pages.
Let's tape them all together!

THIS IS GREAT! See- the Little Engine that Could just rammed Mike Mulligan's Steam Shovel!
WOW! Look what the Poky Little Puppy did to the Cat in the Hat!
HA-HA! I can't wait to do this with all the books at home!

Dad! Are you taking down the safety gate?
Alice, you're four. You don't need it any-more.
The gate was for me?
Yup.

PETEY!
The safety gate was not a last desperate defense against zombies.
What? They didn't take it down, did they?

Why are there signs on every-thing in the classroom?
It's probably the end of the world.
CENTER
Why are there signs on every-thing in the classroom?
Miss Bliss is mock-ing us because we can't read.
Why are there signs on every-thing in the classroom?
They're for Parents' Back-To School Night
I like your answer best.
Thanks! I use it a lot.
R. thompson

Tonight your parents will all come here to Blisshaven Preschool.

And they'll sit right in your chair!
R. Thompson
Both parents at once? Can we come watch that?
Woo. And my dad's not a small man, either.

You should see what he can do to a plastic lawn chair.
So our parents are coming here to play some grotesque version of musical chairs?
And we can't watch?

Thank you all for coming to Parents' Back-to-School Night! I have a treat for you. I've hung the children's self-portraits on our wall. Can you find *your* child without reading the names?

Parents, please enjoy the juice & cookies while we go through the information packets I've prepared for you...

On page 64 is our Hygiene Component, "Strategies of Hand-Washing," with a chart on "The Sleeve," Issues of Nose-Blowing.
Which page?
-YAWN-
R. Thompson

On page 142 is "Naptime Goals & Objectives; Toward a Rested Development."
You've got a juice mustache.
Hey! There's a crankiness index!
Z Z Z

-YAWN- Did I miss anything?
R. Thompson

You missed the part where everybody was staring at you because you were snoring.
Oh-

Z
Miss Bliss didn't notice until you slipped off the tiny chair the first time.

My Dad drives a teeny-weeny car.
He says it's a Honda-Tonka mix, with a little Cuisinart.
BEEP!

Once he left it in the driveway and it got mixed up with my toys.
We found it in my sandbox.
For my midlife crisis, I want a monster truck.
Of course.
Sorry, Daddy.

I enjoy watching your Dad get out of his car.
Once he got it stuck on his foot and walked around like that for an hour till my Mom told him.

My Mom drives a van of a color so neutral it does not occur in nature.
Sometimes it's like one of those animal shows on TV where only the mother can recognize her young-
Beep!
There she is!

My Mom has a great maternal instinct.
Are any of you kids mine?
I'm not a kid. I'm Mrs. Grace Ritter and I want to go to the Safeway.

Mine.
Mine.
Mine.
No.
Every day I test the boundaries of my domain.
Of course. We learn by grabbing.

Dill, want to climb on the big jungle gym?
Alice! Are you joking?
I've heard of kids getting lost in that thing for years at a time!

Then one day emerging unexpectedly from a tube slide, their bodies stooped with age, their gray beards brushing the ground...
Is that a yes or a no?

What is that?
A sign about a lady.
SALE
R. thompson

Why're there balloons?
Maybe it's her birthday.
LE
FRANKIE POTTS Realty

Should we get her a present?
Not a scarf. Looks like she's wearing six of 'em already.
I want a sign like that for my birthday.
SALE

Our class guinea pig is so cute! What's your name, guinea pig?
Danders, Mr. Danders.
Though by rights it should be Doctor Danders, if all my years in this class are taken into consideration.

In fact, if you would, mention to Miss Bliss that I'd look very favorably on an honorary degree.
Don't listen to him! He's a resumé-padder!

Ah, perfect!
LI'L STEP

Jeez, that's her worst one yet.
Aw, I think it's cute. She's only 4.
PIZZA 24
DIET PLAN

OW!
And you're bitter because I'll go into a photo album, but you'll just go in the trash!

Photographs! You are SO sentimental.
Yeah? Comic strips are supposed to be funny. You aren't funny.
DIET PLAN

Ah, I hope your magnet degausses.
BE QUIET, OR I'LL EAT YOU!
Oh, I wouldn't do that.
DIET PLAN
R. thompson

I hadn't realized guinea pigs hate hermit crabs.
Oh, yes-
R. Thompson

In the wild, guinea pigs and hermit crabs are deadly enemies. They engage in vicious battles lasting for days.

I saw one of those on a TV nature show. It was real pathetic.
OH! IF THESE BARS DID NOT CONSTRAIN ME YOU'D SEE SOMETHING EPIC!
HA!

She's actually a doggie chew-toy that I rescued. If I hadn't, she would've been ripped to shreds, like on those animal TV shows with all the lions and the blood and guts all over the place.

R. Thompson

I've got a hammer, so now I can fix things!
Here, take a look at my jack-in-the-box.
BOOP BOOP

I'd say your spring is too tight.
No, I like that part. I just hate the tune it plays!
A TINY CLOWN DROPPED ON MY HEAD! GET IT OFF ME SOMEBODY!
R. Thompson

Let's see what I can do for your jack-in-the-box.
Thanks, Beni.

First, a few exploratory taps.
Ah, here's the problem.
PING
PING

He's so handy.
I'd love to see what he could do with a saw or a nail gun.
BANG
BANG
BANG
BANG
R. thompson

How's the jack-in-the-box now, Alice?
It sounds much better, Beni. Thank you.
BHUB UHB UGK

No problem.
You know, my dad's been having trouble with his lawn mower.

Let's go take a look at it!
Hey, Petey! Beni fixed this thing so that awful clown won't jump out.
UGK OOP OOP
Still, let's not tempt fate.
R. Thompson

AGH-
EWGH-
YUCK!
They're just cicadas, Alice. You're the one who's not afraid of anything.
ZT

But these're bugs, with all those legs. EURGH. They're scary.
Do what I do. Construct a distancing fantasy as a coping mechanism.

Do WHAT?
I simply imagine the cicadas are my own private army of tiny Mothras all eager to do my bidding! They're instantly transformed from red-eyed monsters into my little pals!
TZT

Ah.

SOON
What is—
Look! I've dressed the cicadas in cute little dresses made of paper napkins! HA-HA! Who could be scared of that? Help me write their names on them.
TZ
This one's Darlene.

LATER.
YIKES! They've found cicadas around here wearing strange paper outfits, suggesting a possible species of super-intelligent cicadas. And they all had girls' names, too.
EWGH! Don't tell the kids. It'll just scare them.
METRO
SUPERBUG?
R. Thompson

R. Thompson

I can control bees with my mind!
I can't even control myself with my mind.

Show us how you control bees with your mind.
BEE—

DO A LOOP-DE-LOOP.

Ah!
Will you use your new-found power for good or evil?
I'll spread it around to even things out.
R. Thompson

Now make the bee do something useful.
BEE-GO FIX ME A BOLOGNA SANDWICH

BUZZ

RUN!
RUN!

Hey, that's a june bug! Ha! Don't I feel silly.
No wonder it tried to sting us.
R. Thompson

For today's feat of Bee Mind Control, I will attempt TWO BEES at once!

Kevin's dog found something really disgusting and he's eating it!

My 15 minutes are up, my star has dwindled, my fame has fled.
Where's this dog at?
R. Thompson

Look, they're digging for new houses.
Is that how they get new houses? Dig for them like potatoes?

I don't know. I'll go ask the guy wearing a hat.
Ok.

He patted me on the head and said I'm cute. He... he tousled my hair!
A sure sign of ignorance in an adult. He must not know either.
R. Thompson

Are you going to push me or not?
I can't reach you! The under-swing trench is too deep!

Go find me a taller kid then.
I can't get out! Help! I'm stuck in an under-swing trench!
R. Thompson

Children, we have a special guest!
Let's welcome Timmy Fretwork!
Hi, kids!
twang
I'm gonna play my banjo & sing some songs for you! The first song's about a farmer who had him a dog named "Bingo"— Yes? Question?
I have a dog.
Nara! That's not a question!
I have a dog, too!
I have two cats!
I have a dog!
My dog runs fast!
My cat sleeps on my bed!
One time I saw my dog eat snow!
One time I put a snow-globe in the microwave and pushed "Hot Dog."
OUR TIME-OUT CORNER
Every time that woman tries to cram culture down our throats, this happens.

Mom, I don't know what to draw for Dill's birthday card.
Well, think of something special about Dill.
He's always got gum in his hair.
His parents let a four-year-old chew gum?
ALICE'S
ALICE'S

No, he walks under restaurant tables a lot.
Just draw some flowers.
ALICE'S

Do you want me to walk you over to Dill's party?
MOM. It's right across the street.

Be careful crossing.
MOM. There's no traffic.

Do you have Dill's birthday present?
MOM. Yes!

If they start spinning the bottle, you come right home.
DAD!

Hi, Mister Wedekind.
Hi, Alice! Is that present for me?
No, it's Dill's. For his birthday.
Ooh! Is it a bicycle?
No, it's a book. Excuse me.
Sure looks like a bicycle! Ha ha!

Ha ha ha ha ha ha ha ha ha!
Ha ha. Ha ha.
Hm.
p t hompson

Happy Birthday, Dill.
Hi, Alice! Here's your goodie bag.
R. Thompson

Where is everybody?
They, um, they...

Did you give them their goodie bags and they all went home?
Uh-huh.

You confused them! You're supposed to give out the goodie bags LAST!
I'm not very good at this—

What do we do now?
Here's a birthday party game! I'll put a sticker on your head.

Why?
Now I'll put one on my head, and we'll ask questions to find out what's on them!

Okay. Why have you got a duck stuck on your head?
I don't know. What are you doing with a frog stuck on yours?

That was fun.
Wait, who won? The winner gets a plastic whistle.
R. Thompson

Nobody else was there, the games were boring, his mom made his birthday cake a CARROT CAKE. Ick.

And look what's in the goodie bag— a little package of soy sauce, some frilly toothpicks and a teenie-weenie bottle of shampoo.

Alice, catch me so I don't fall on my head.
Okay.
WHEE!
YAHOO!

YIKES
WHOA, MAN!
WOW!

I-YI-YI YI-YI-YI-
OOF
I SEE LIGHT! I SEE LIGHT!
GEEZ THAT WAS GREAT!

Where'd you get the sandwich?
My Mom made it. Are you going to fall on your head or not?

You know what I wish?
What?

I wish that when I got mad I could pull my own head off and throw it at people.

What would you do for a head?
I'd grow a new one each time.
So the place would be full of old Alice heads?
Would they all keep talking? Please say no.

Alice, what are you going to be for Halloween?
Is Halloween the one with the hearts?

No, it's when you dress up and get candy. Last year you were a cow!
A cow? Did people laugh and point?

Well, yes. You were so cute.
That explains the flashbacks I keep having.

Tell me the story of Halloween.
It doesn't really have a story.
It has to have a story.
It's just for fun-
It's to placate the zombies.
Oh. Okay.
Petey! Stop with the zombies and go to bed.
R. Thompson

I want to be this for Halloween.
What?

It's a crayon sharpener shaped like a cat. It's my favorite thing!
I'll tape it to my head.

There! Tell me I don't look scary.
I don't think you've grasped the possibilities of Halloween.
R. Thompson

I want to be this for Halloween.
What?

Princess Fairyqueen, Queen of all the Fairy Princesses. She's my favorite thing.

Um, Okay. We can make a costume—
And the wings have to really fly. And the wand really shoots a death ray.
R. Thompson

I'm going like this for Halloween.
Boo!

BOO!

It's dignified yet expressive.

How about "Boo," no exclamation point?
Even better!
R. Thompson

Princess Fairyqueen! She's the star of those TV cartoons! Plus she's got books, DVDs, CDs, a weekly magazine, video games, lunchboxes, snacks, millions of toys—

She's on breakfast cereals, linens, shower curtains, sleepwear, active wear, athletic shoes, bandages, hats, scarves, baby items, a vast interactive web site, an airmail stamp in Pago Pago, a limited-edition SUV—

I'm going like this for Halloween.
BOO
BOO

BOO

It says "Boo."
YAGH!

Four-year-olds shouldn't know about sarcasm.
MOM! HELP! YAGH!
BOO
R. Thompson

Petey, you're really going like that for Halloween?
Yes.
BOO

I don't want to dress up as some-thing people will stare at.
Boo

And I don't like rubber masks. They smell and I can't see out of them.
Boo.

If that's what he wants.
And yet he keeps asking to wear his viking helmet to school.

Don't get too far ahead, Alice.
I want everyone to see me!

NARA! What're You?
I'm Princess Fairyqueen!
R. Thompson

I already did all the houses on our street.
No! BUT! I'M! No! BUT! I'M!

EEEE-YAGH!
Ooh! A scary monster!

Hey guys! How was trick or treating?
Awful.
M
BOO

Everybody thought I was Boo Radley. "Look! It's Boo Radley!" So finally I asked, "WHO'S BOO RADLEY?"
R. Thompson
Boo

I felt like such a bone-head.
Aw, Petey...
I unwrapped most of my candy so it'll be faster to eat. Help me with the rest—
M
Boo

Why is our tree tied up?
So it won't jump out of the ground and chase you.

When trees are young, they don't know how to stand still.
Oh.

You can't get me! NYAA!
Taunting the inanimate is cruel.
R. Thompson

I have to do a stupid leaf collection for preschool.
I kept the one I made in preschool.

Why?
I keep my entire output arranged by date. Here: "LEAF COLLECTION."

COUGH -GAH- DUST!
No! That was to be the centerpiece of my college admission!
R. Thompson

AHem.

- And he said there were people behind the mirror with cameras and clipboards watching me the whole time!
PETEY! Did you really tell your sister that?
R. Thompson

Well, MAYBE there are!

Why do I have to make a Leaf Collection?
Miss Bliss wants you to learn about Nature and Shapes and Colors.

Do you know Shapes and Colors, Dad?
Of course! I'm a grown-up!

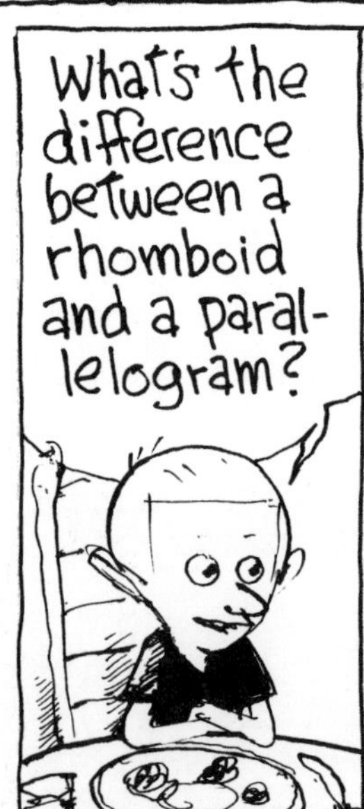
What's the difference between a rhomboid and a parallelogram?

Well, Petey, that's a controversial subject—
AND WHO GIVES A BIG FAT HOOT, I wanna know.
P. Thompson

You should thank me for helping you collect leaves.
Why does Miss Bliss make us do this stuff?
Leaves are boring.
HEY! A PIZZA COUPON!
Ooh! Put that in my Leaf Collection!
No. It doesn't count!
It'll be for extra credit! C'mon, Miss Bliss says thriftiness is good!
No! It's MINE! You owe me, Alice!
R. Thompson

Did you help Alice with her Leaf Collection?
Yeah, and look! I found a pizza coupon!

Petey, that expired in August.
I know. I keep them.

You keep old coupons?
I have a binder full. It's labeled "Missed Opportunities."

I am very pleased with everyone's Leaf Collection! They do Blisshaven Preschool PROUD!

You each get a star, a sticker and a leaf-shaped cookie!

WOW! I love leaf collecting!
I want to be a leaf collector!
I hear they drive GIANT VACUUM TRUCKS!
REALLY? Why wasn't that mentioned in the lesson plan?
R. Thompson

Our class guinea pig is so cute!
But he never does anything.
Ah-

That is the way of the guinea pig. We respond to stimuli by becoming small lumps of inertia, implacable in our stillness.
R. Thompson

Tell me more of this "inertia." I like the sound of it.
I dunno. It smacks of the "bump-on-a-logism" my mom so roundly condemns.

Tell me more about guinea pigs!
Of course!
The Great Behemoth Guinea Pigs of the Ice Age would suddenly freeze, motionless, when attacked.
HEY!

Frustrated, the hunters would soon quit.
I don't feel challenged as a hunter-gatherer.
So you see, lethargy is often the best response.
I'm finally learning something in school!
R-Thompson

Today we're going to use a new communication tool in class! It's called a "Talking Stick."
OOH!

See? It has ribbons and glitter on it to make it special! whoever holds it speaks while the rest of the class listens attentively.

Who has something to say? Alice? Here, you may be the first to use the Talking Stick!
Yes, Miss Bliss!

OKAY, STAND BACK! I'M DOING THE TALKING! DON'T TRY ANYTHING FUNNY 'CAUSE I HAVE A STICK!
R. thompson

Miss Bliss, do you swing it like a hammer or like a baseball bat?
Thank you, Alice, you may sit down please!

Maybe Dill has something to say and he'd like to hold the Talking Stick.
Yes, Miss Bliss!

HI, I'M MR. STICKY THE TALKING STICK! I'M SURE GLAD I'M NOT STILL GROWING OUT OF SOME STUPID TREE-
R. Thompson

WITH A COUPLE OF STUPID BIRDS SITTING ON M-
GRAB

She took it away because "Mr. Sticky" is a dumb name.
PHOOEY.

I think this class still does not know the purpose of the Talking Stick.

The Talking Stick is about deference, respect and taking turns, the keys to civilized discourse.
RThompson

Look! I made my own Talking Stick!
Me, too, out of a popsicle stick!
Mine has a ribbon!
Mine has a ribbon and glitter! So my Talking Stick is the loudest!

Alice, look. Here's how you can write your own name.
R. Thompson

There! LS! It's like code for Alice!
REALLY? Let me try–
LS

LS
I did it! HA HA HA!

Will just anyone be able to read this? Am I at risk of identity theft?
There's always that danger.

I can write my own name, see? LS! ALICE!
Do it again!
CHALK

R. THOMPSON
It gets better each time!
HA HA! MORE!

Dang, I'm out of chalk.
I think we're lost, too.

Alice, why are you writing "57" everywhere?
DAD. It's "LS." It's my name. ALICE.
LS
He was looking at it upside down, you know.
Is he not too, um, bright?
I think creative writing confuses him.
LS
R. Thompson

Alice! Look at the chalk dust all over you!
I've been writing my name!
LS
LS
LS

BATH TIME!
HEY!

Oh, how we writers suffer.
I hear the same thing happened to Herman Melville, whoever he is.
R. thompson

Petey, what's that?
It's my school project on Thanksgiving. It didn't go so well.
C-

Why?
Instead of the FIRST Thanksgiving, I did a diorama of the THIRD Thanksgiving, when they were all getting on each other's nerves.
C-

See, they're standing around in an awkward silence. And look, everyone hates the stuffing, and the turkey came out dry.

The Native Americans are sitting at a separate table because all the pilgrims are talking about football. And who cares about that?

Ha! It's great! I always love your work!
Well, my teacher says it didn't fall within the parameters of the assignment. Now it just makes me cringe.
C-
R. Thompson

Would it help if I took it outside and ran over it with my tricycle?
Sure. Back up over it a few times, too.

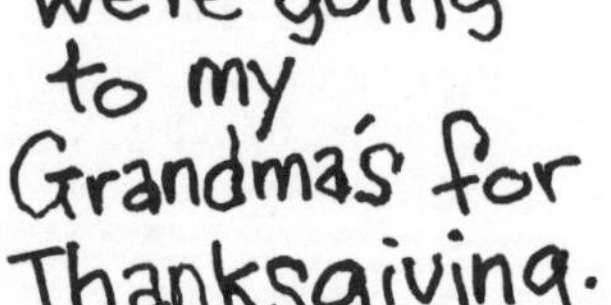
We're going to my Grandma's for Thanksgiving.

She has a dog I'm scared of named Big Shirley.

Petey says Big Shirley probably ate Grandpa.

My grandma tells filthy jokes in Spanish.
Petey also says Grandma puts dog kibble in the stuffing.
R. Thompson

My Grandma used to wave at traffic all day.

Then she got tired of traffic. Now she throws deviled eggs at it.
R thompson

Grandma's got a good arm, too.
Grandma! It's us!
You people need a more distinctive car.

Hi, Grandma! We're here for Thanksgiving Dinner!

Show her the food.
Look, Grandma! Food! FOOOOOD! We bring food! Friends!

Alice! Stop THAT!
You can come in, but those better not be beets.

I didn't clean off the dining room table. I always eat in here.
This is real cozy, Grandma!
R. Thompson

Can we turn on the TV and watch Christmas commercials?
DOWN! DOWN! BAD! DOWN, BIG SHIRLEY! BAD DOG!

While we clean up the dishes, why don't you play in Grandma's yard?
But-

Are there people buried under these things?
Only under the windmills, but watch your step.
R. Thompson

How was dinner at your Grandma's?
Okay...

Except I spilled gravy on my head avoiding Big Shirley.

So I had to take a bath in Grandma's scary bathtub.

I still smell like her crabapple-lye shampoo.
My Grandma smells like the bingo hall.
R. Thompson

Petey, what're those?
They're "comic strips," examples of a mighty, yet dying art form.

Read this one to me.
Well, see the cat says-

Is he happy or sad?
I don't know yet.

I think he's sad.
Okay. He says—

He's sad because the last cat here is eating pie.
No! He-

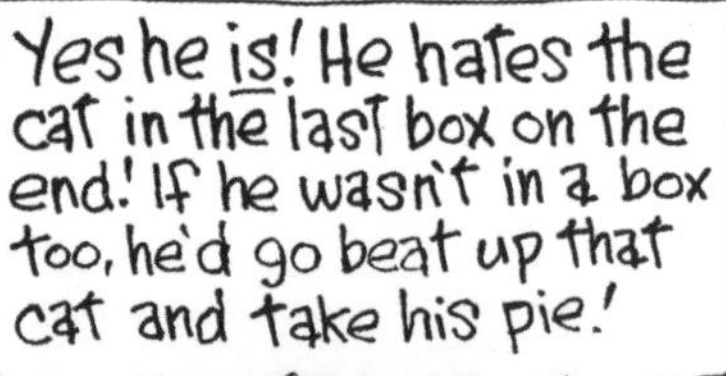
Yes he is! He hates the cat in the last box on the end! If he wasn't in a box too, he'd go beat up that cat and take his pie!

R. Thompson

ALICE! IT'S ALL THE SAME CAT! SEE? THEY'RE ALL HIM!

Actually, I think he's a girl cat.
Maybe it's just as well comic strips are a dying art form.

Shall we try a pixie cut, Alice?
What's that?

It's when your hair is so short your head looks like a wheel of cheese with mold on it.

PETEY.
I love cheese! Can we do the moldy pixie head cheese look?
R. Thompson

Mom, do you really know how to cut hair?
Sure!

She always cuts my hair!
She cuts mine when she can find it!

ALICE! GET BACK HERE!
ZING
R. Thompson

Why can't I have long hair?
R. Thompson

Because...?
What?

Because when you had long hair you kept flossing your teeth with it, remember?

I still think that's a good idea.
That's why you can't have long hair.

There, all done! See?
Did you find anything in my hair?

Like what?
Plastic farm animals, some doll shoes, crayons, those old earrings you gave me, candy-

You lost all that in your hair?
Or it might all be under my car seat, like last time.
R. Thompson

ALICE! Are you eating spaghetti with your hands?
Hey! If I eat it with my feet it makes my socks turn orange!

A-HA-HAAA!

My comedy is too cutting-edge for her.
R. Thompson

I think my mom is stalking me—
Why, Marcus?

Every little thing I do, she takes a picture and glues it in a scrapbook.
Uh-Oh.

I'm barely 4 and she's already up to "Marcus, Volume 36."
I'll bet she's compiling evidence for future use against you.
R. Thompson

Let's try your Jack-in-the-Box again.
BOOP DA BOOP DA BOOP
It's a little slow.
R. Thompson
BING
SMEK

That was creepy.
Yeah. It's been giving me nightmares.

Alice! Stop gobbling your food so fast.
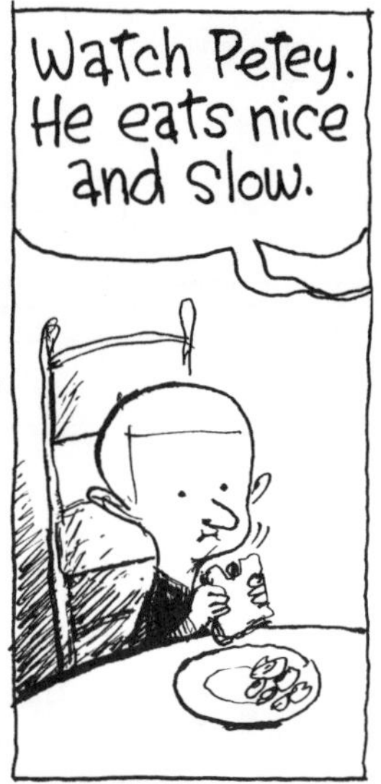
Watch Petey. He eats nice and slow.

I don't like the bites to collide going down...

They might pile up dangerously in the stomach.
I should watch that?
Watch. Don't listen.
R. Thompson

My mom's van is "in the shop."
She's selling her van?

Huh?
If it's in the shop, it must be for sale.

But I've got a stash of old candy and fast food hidden under the backseat!
Oh, that'll sell fast.
R. Thompson

My dad drove me to school in his little tiny car.
How was that?
Hey, Dad! Drive into the classroom and do donuts around Miss Bliss, OK?

It was no fun at all.

I had this dream last night-
I hate hearing about somebody's boring dream.

You were in it.
ME? What was I doing?

Complaining about being in somebody's boring dream.
Well, yeah.
RThompson

ABABU.

BABU OOPA!
NO-

OBABU OOPA SPOO!
GAH!
R. Thompson

Strange babies keep attacking me.
Petey, I don't think-
It's because your head's shaped like a rattle.

ABOO.
No.

BUMBA.
GAH!

ABOOMBA!

Babies pushing strollers are a MENACE.
Look out, I think it's circling for another attack.
R Thompson

Come here, Alice! Tell me about your day!
What? DADDY!! QUIT!

Tell me what you did at preschool!
DAAAAAD! DON'T! HEE HEE HEE HEE!
BOUNCE
BOUNCE

Tell me the best thing that happened today.
DAAAAAAD! HEE HEE HEE HA HA!
BOUNCE
BOUNCE

Tell me quick or you'll bounce through the ceiling!
HA HAHA HAHA!
-BOUNCE
BOUNCE

Whoops. Uh-oh.
CRASH
ALICE?!
OOOOOWHAAAAAA

He did that to me when I was six and I didn't get a milk shake.
You're just trying to cheer me up.
R. Thompson

Excuse us.
Make room, Petey.

Twins! Aren't they cute?

No, they don't have a "hive mind," and it was rude of you to ask.
Their eyes— staring at me.
R. Thompson

BABA GOB!
Um. GAH.

That baby gave me a wet cracker.
Ew. Babies are so low to the ground I'll bet they're all germy.

It's stuck! AGH. I can't get it off of me!
It's attached itself to you like one of those parasite things on a TV animal show.
R. Thompson

I don't know what to draw. I can't think of anything to draw. There's nothing to draw.
Draw me!

You? Okay.

There.
Why'd you make me look so mean?

I can't stand people who tell me what to do.
R. Thompson

Oh boy! I found popcorn in my pocket!
What?

It's from when I went to the movies last night and I spilled some.
Ha ha! I love finding popcorn in my pocket!

Or maybe from when I went to the movies last month. Chew chew chew.
Did you find enough for everybody?
BAP
BAP
BAP
R. Thompson

HEY, MOM!
Careful, Alice. I'm wearing-

my new Christmas sweater.
WAP

Alice? Are you all right?

Honey, I'd pick you up, but I can't bend over.
OW.
R. THOMPSON

Wow, that's your Christmas sweater?
Yup! Watch-

CHUG CHUG CHUG CHUG CHUG CHUG CHUG

CHUG CHUG CHUG TOOT TOOT TOOT

How can a sweater do that?
It's toasty warm, too!

Is this one of those dumb holiday comedies where the dad does stupid things?
I hope so.
Ssh.

I'll bet that Christmas tree falls over on him.
I hope so.
Ssh.

He's not going to climb the ladder.
YAY! Climb the ladder!
Oh NO! I lost a mitten in the tub of popcorn!
ALICE!

Don't worry, Alice. It'll be okay.
It's my favorite fuzzy mitten.
Ik.
We'll find it.

You were eating popcorn with your fuzzy mittens on?
YES.
Ssh.

Hey! If this was the movie, Daddy would accidentally eat the mitten!
SSH.
Eat the mitten, Daddy!
Who are you people?
R. Thompson

Watch Alice's breath in the cold air!

She's Queen of the Mouth Breathers!
It's like she's an undersea volcanic vent!
I've always said so.
R thompson

Okay, Petey, where shall we put these lights?

In that shrub like always?
You see how my theory of minimalist landscaping makes such decisions easy?
R. Thompson

Ok, let's put the lights in the shrub.
There's a string of lights here already.

Oh, yeah?
A couple of 'em. No, lots of them! And look-Sports equipment!
R. thompson

Guess we didn't-
A Frisbee, a catcher's mitt. Hey, an old news-paper.

-Clean it out ever.
"Nixon Resigns." What on earth can that mean?

Is it done, Daddy? Is it done?
No, Alice. You can't rush this.

You have to use care and a good eye when arranging Christmas lights in a shrub. See? Like this, and this.
R. Thompson

Is it done, Daddy? Is it done?
Yup.
Can I go in now?

Let's all step out on the street so we get the total effect of our Christmas lights.

Well, **I** can't see them.

There.
Ooh!
Can I go in now?
R. thompson

We like your hat, Mr. Otterloop!
Dad, do your trick!
OK.
AAAND—
SPIN

TA-DAH!
Does he ever get stuck in it backwards?
I don't know. Hey, Dad, try it again!
R. Thompson

Should we get a photo of them on Santa's lap?
I guess.
Im not going to actually sit on his lap.

There's a Precious Memory Package with 25 photo cards, 20 8x10s...
I'll stand to one side with an air of quiet reserve.
Take off your hat, Alice.
NO.
A VISIT WITH SANTA

Six photo mugs, six photo magnets, five photo ornaments, four photo beer koozies, a photo mousepad...
Alice.
No. I like the hat on. Santa's wearing his hat.

All for $49.95.
Your turn, kids! Smile big!
HEY!

Aw, look! Grandma will love these!
Dibs on a beer koozie.
If you'd gotten the Precious Memory Deluxe Package, Grandma would get a tattoo.
HUMPH.

So what are "Sugar Plums"? Some kind of bug, right?
It's a breakfast cereal.

It's a rash you get if you eat too much candy.
No. Sugar Plums are tiny demons, half vampire bat and half circus clown, who invade the dreams of the unwary.

That's why they danced on the guy's head in that poem.
Dill always has the best answers!
Oh, he's a wonder.

A soccer ball? Why did Santa bring me a **soccer ball?**
Maybe he thinks you should try soccer!

Can he do that? Can Santa take it into his head to give me something I don't want?

That's too much power if you ask me.
The way he makes toys that're impossible to open, you know Santa has a dark side.
LITTLE MISS FUNSY
R. Thompson

Aw! Look how Alice is sitting!

She's got her feet stuck out to the side like little kids do! Ha ha ha!

Sometimes they just make me so self-conscious.
What I do is, when I catch myself doing something "cute," I freeze, then back away quickly.
R. Thompson

Where'd you go for the holidays, guinea pig?
To the house of one of your classmates whose name escapes me.

His mother had "allergies", so I spent the entire week in the garage. It was awful: dark, cold and filled with thousands of ludicrous "handyman" gadgets.
R. Thompson

Whoops. I gotta go finish coloring something.
I'm thankful enough for the hospitality, but I still smell like a lawn mower.

Pop
Pop
POP
POP
Pop
Pop

Oh! Is that the new model?
Yes, I got it for Christmas.
Pop

Mine isn't as noisy. Have they improved it?
They increased the number of balls and they enlarged the spring! Isn't it sweet?

That was the most adult conversation I've ever had.
Wasn't it boring?
Pop

BOMP

Petey? Think fast.
ALICE! You're supposed to say that FIRST. REAL LOUD.

The finer points of sports elude me.
Did we win?
Throw it at him again and find out.
R. Thompson

Did you get that for Christmas?
Yes. Santa brought it.

What is it?
I don't know. I saw it in the store and I felt sorry for it.

It is pretty sad.
Nobody was buying it. It was pathetic. So I asked Santa for it.

I wish **I** had one.
That's the only one there is.

Petey, what is New Year's?
It's when the year starts all over again.
LITTLE NEURO

All over again? Just like before?
No, it's new, so new things happen.
LITTLE NEURO

Everything starts new? EVERY-THING?
YES, Alice.
LITTLE

My name is now Sonia, and I'm an eight-foot-tall rabbit who's really cute.
Okey-dokey, Sonia.
LITTLE NEURO

It's New Year's, so everything is new, so I'm now a giant rabbit named Sonia.
We get to be some-thing new?
Great! I'll be a grocery cart-herder!

I'll herd stray carts into long lines and push them around the parking lot.

I want to be that too!
We'll all be cart-herds!
We'll live at the grocery store and eat like kings!
R. Thompson

We're going to be grocery cart-herds this year!
What?
R. Thompson

We'll live at the grocery store and herd the stray carts into long lines! People will love us for it!

We'll have the run of the cereal aisle!
Oooh!
Will everyone please leave my room in a brisk yet orderly manner?

Uh-oh...
We're in a Christmas tree grave-yard.
I've got the creeps! I've got the creeps!
RUN!
R. Thompson

Hold your breath.
Here comes Petey.
Hold it...hold it...

Okay, BREATHE!
AGH! GODZILLA!
R. Thompson

Mine.

Mine.

Mine.
No.

I almost scored a TV remote.
Ooh, the one that got away.
R. Thompson

My life intersects with Alice's just enough to be surreal.
Hmm?

Daddy's getting on my nerves. He's always right there.
It's 'cause our house is so small. If he'd get a better job, we could move someplace bigger.
30 PIECE PUZZLE
REMORSE COMICS
R. Thompson

Alice, honey, do you feel all right? Let's feel your forehead.

Here, feel her forehead.
Hmm.

Feels a little hot.
Poor baby.
Can I try?

I think you have to go home now, Dill.
Ok, but my brother is a large-animal vet, so I do have a medical background.
R. Thompson

Alice, if you'll blow your nose, you'll feel better.
Sniff.
R. Thompson
Blow.
Sniff.
BLOW.
SNIFF.
BL
SNI
Pretend your nose is a water pistol.
SNORt
Petey! You have the makings of a great doctor!
OK, but no shots.

I'll give you some medicine for your fever, Alice.
R.Thompson

What flavor is it?
Ummm... "Cotton Candy." Ick.

ICK?
No! It's cotton candy flavor! Yum!

You SAID ICK! YOU SAID ICK!!
I meant to say yum! Look, it's bright pink! How bad can it be?

The duck loses his favorite hat, it's blue, so he goes all over asking everyone, have you seen my hat, it's blue, and the cow says no, and the pig says no, and the dog says no, **so** the duck goes home and closes the door and there's the hat on the back of the door!

Today at preschool, since Alice stayed home, nobody yelled, nobody threw dirt at recess, nobody hogged all the crayons. It was the most boring day ever.

R. Thompson

Hi, Dill.
Hi, Alice. I made a get-well card for you. See?

It's a giant germ stomping on your head!

It's the nicest card I've ever gotten that didn't have money in it.
Remember that in 20 years when I ask you to marry me.
R. Thompson

Look! Up in the window!
It's Alice!
Uh-oh.

I guess she's not sick anymore.
Maybe she'll come out and play!
But she always throws dirt!

Act like we're having fun! She'll get mad and come outside!
OOF! OOF! MY HAT!
What if she throws dirt at us from way up there? RUN! RUN!
R. Thompson

Can I go to preschool today?
No, I'm keeping you home one more day.
But the children miss me!
Absence makes the heart grow fonder.

They'll forget who I am! They'll say, who are you? I'll be the "NEW KID."
Alice, are you getting a fever again?
R. thompson

What sounds good for dinner?
Those noodles shaped like plumbing.

Macaroni again?
Can we try the cheese samples? Can we weigh fruit? Can we look at the lobster tank?

You are feeling better.
Daddy told me the lobsters sometimes escape and chase people. Can we do that?
R. Thompson

Daddy, can I go to preschool today?
Yup! Mom'll take you.
Ooh, I'll bet Miss Bliss lets me sit in the Very Special Chair!
It's painted gold!
VERY SPECIAL

Those who sit in it rule as kings! All at Blisshaven Preschool bend to their will!
Megalomania scares me first thing in the morning.
R. Thompson

Hi, Miss Bliss, I'm back! Can I sit in the Very Special Chair?
I'm glad you're feeling better, Alice..

But it's Nara's birthday, so she's sitting in the Very Special Chair.
!

A whole week out sick, wasted.
Oh cheer up. Nara's mom made cupcakes!
And look how blue the icing is!
R. thompson

How was your first day back?
It was Nara's birthday, so she got to sit in the Very Special Chair.

I was sick for a week. You'd think I'd get the chair.
I see Nara's mom made cupcakes.

I don't want it. I'm just keeping it as an aid to sulking.
Yet you managed to eat all the icing off it.
R Thompson

Our class guinea pig is so cute! What's your name, guinea pig?
Danders. Mr. Danders, though it might well be Dr. Danders.

If ever anyone earned an honorary doctorate, it would be me.

For I've spent my life here, in the groves of academe, breathing the tangy scent of Play-Doh, the humid reek of the coat cubbies.
Attending to the soft scratch of crayon on paper, the lulling drone of story time.

With the knowledge I've gleaned, I could've excelled in many fields.
DANDERS
–
POET,
JURIST,
SURGEON,
BANJO
VIRTUOSO

But no! My duties lie here! Generations of Blisshaven Preschool students have looked to me, faithful Danders, for a hearty "GWEEP" of encouragement when learning palls and their weary heads nod!
GWEEP!

That GWEEPing noise was you? I thought it was Miss Bliss' stomach.
Alas! Do all my efforts go unrecognized?
R. Thompson

Alice, listen to me, please. You've got to stop grabbing things and yelling, "MINE!"

Because it's very— Wait! Don't do that!

Don't spin around when I'm talking to you!
Why?

It's rude. It shows you aren't paying attention.

Now listen. I don't—

Alice! You did it again! I want you to look at me while I'm talking. Okay?

OKAY, ALICE?
O-KAY

It's further proof that people actually exist only when I'm looking at them.
I can't hear you!

That's a nice paper towel roll, Dill.
Thanks. I had to work hard to get it.

You can't imagine how many messy spills I caused to use up all the paper towels.

Really?
The final one was epic. A glass full of apple juice. It took like a hundred towels.
R. Thompson

Why do they have to bury the rolls under so many paper towels?
Adults are so wasteful.

Should I use my paper towel roll to look through or to yell through?
Do BOTH!

I can't do both. These things are delicate.
Sure you can! Here-

Don't grab it!
I'll show you how to use a paper towel roll-OOPS
RThompson

NO! It fell in a puddle!
OH! MOP IT UP! GET SOME PAPER TOWELS!

Look at my paper Towel roll! You ruined it!
I'm so, sorry! How can I make it up to you?

I worked s-so hard for this!
Here, take one of these-

What is it?
A rock with a smiley face drawn on it!

You made this?
I've made millions of them! Rocks are so glum, it drives me crazy.
R. Thompson

You draw happy faces on little rocks?
Yes, it's my way of spreading cheer!
I draw a happy face on a rock, then release it into the wild for everyone to enjoy!
You're such a good person.

Why do I keep feeling like I'm being stared at and laughed at?
Petey, you're going to be late for school again.

How many little rocks have you drawn smiley faces on?
It's hard to say...
R. Thompson

Maybe ten billion! I hope that soon they'll cover the Earth in a vast army of tiny, cute cheerful rocks!
That'd be great!

I've found a rock in my shoe that's laughing at me.
You must have happy feet!

LOOK! A SNOW-FLAKE!
There it goes!
RUN!
CATCH IT!
FASTER!
IT'S GETTING AWAY!
R. Thompson

ALICE! It's time to come in!
HE ATE IT!
DADDY! COUGH IT UP!
SLAP HIM ON THE BACK, QUICK!

Today we're going to try an exciting new art form!
Miss Bliss, my sister wears a uniform to school. Can we wear uniforms, too?

No. It's called ORIGAMI! Please take a sheet of paper.
If we get uniforms, will they come with hats, too?

No. Now fold along with me as we make an origami duck!
If we get uniforms and hats, would we be issued weapons, too?
FOLD
FOLD
FOLD
FOLD
FOLD

No. Fold this here, this over here-
FOLD
FOLD

And, voila! A DUCK!
This cootie-catcher is lethal at a distance of 20 feet!

Every time she tries something new, this happens.
TIME-OUT CORNER
And I got a paper cut.
R. thompson

Alice.

Alice. I don't think that man wants you staring at him while he eats.
Yeah, no wonder. He's got pancake syrup all over his beard.
Let me see.
R thompson

I dropped my blue crayon!
Go find it quick.

Wow, it's like a whole new world down here!

A world of shreds of paper, bent straws old pickle slices, lost french fries-

A world where everything is sticky.
You're not eating things down there, are you?

Good night, Alice.
Sing the Snuggy Song!

I sang the Snuggy Song. I did the Rock-a-Bye Dance. I did the Big Hugaboo and the Whoopsie Bedtime Pratfall.

It's not enough!
Good night!

My bedtime ritual needs greater elaboration.
Click
R. Thompson

HHHNNNNGGGGGEEEEEEEEEEEE
What's that noise?
My brother Petey is practicing his oboe. That's his new note!

NNGGHKSBPLLLS
What happened to his old note?
Listen - this is the part where he drools!
R. Thompson

Petey will now play his new note on the oboe.
Mmp

MMNG

HEENK
Whew.

His tone is good but his timing is terrible.
Is it over? Should I clap?

My nose is running.
Does your nose run and your feet smell? Uh-oh! You're built upside-down!

AHAHAHAHAHAHAHA HAHAHAHA. HAHAHA. HAHA.

Is Petey taking uncomprehending stare lessons from Alice?
Hm?

My brother says you shouldn't suck mitten juice.
He's right.
Why not?

That stuff'll corrode your innards. It happened to a friend of his.
It happens all the time.

He was rushed to the hospital for innards-replacement surgery. He now digests his food through 20 feet of garden hose.
My cousin has a party balloon instead of a stomach, thanks to mitten juice.
PTOO!

I think I feel sick. I'm going inside.

I'm going in, too. My snowman is all finished.
Mine, too.
Bye.

MITTEN JUICE?
I think she's got it confused with yellow snow.
R. thompson

Dill, what's that thing in your yard?
My brothers are building a trebuchet.

It's like a catapult. It can throw things real far.

They've promised me a ride in it when it's finished!
LUCKY. Can I come, too?
R. Thompson

Dill's brothers are building a trebuchet. Why doesn't Petey build stuff?
Petey made a very nice horse-head bookend for me once.

I keep it up high on the shelf with all my favorite fragile things.
R. Thompson

I pinched my finger doing it, too. See the scar?
Big deal! How many horse-head books do we have anyway?
Alice.

Alice, where are you taking that ice cube tray?
Up to the bathroom.

If you flush an ice cube down the potty before you go to bed, it'll snow that night for sure! I'm going to dump the whole tray in!
R. Thompson

Or you could go to the store and get some bags of party ice–
You may flush one ice cube, Alice.

So flushing an ice cube tonight makes it snow by morning?
Yes, Dad, it's like a science.

And you have to say the rhyme:
"Ice cube, Ice cube, In the pot, Gee, I hope it snows a lot."

Should I do the Magic Ice Cube Dance?
Please don't spoil this by being silly.
FLUSH

This is the best snowman we've ever made!
It's so realistic!

It's a pleasure working with you!
Thanks, it's a- HEY!

DADDY!
Honey, I have to get to work.
R. Thompson

Grunt.
Oof.
FLIP
Ah!
R. Thompson

That was great.
This morning my Mom had to push him into it with a broom.

Today we'll be making beautiful Valentines to share with our parents!
Ooh!

We'll use construction paper, glitter, glue and cotton balls. And remember, Creativity plus Neatness equals Art!

Beni, please be careful using the glue. Kevin, don't wave the scissors.

Alice, not so much glitter. Dillon, keep your shoes on. Marcus, stop that. COUGH.

Nara, not in your hair. COUGH. Not in Alice's hair either. COUGH COUGH.

COUGH. All right, we should be COUGH finished COUGH. Please put your COUGH on the COUGH COUGH COUGH.

Then Miss Bliss kept on coughing and had to go to the doctor to be treated for acute glitterlung.
Aw, the poor woman! You should make her a card.
R. Thompson

What's that big wall?
It's to keep the traffic out.

Otherwise, the endless stream of cars would rise up and overwhelm the whole neighborhood.
CUL DE SAC

Aren't you glad we're on high ground?
Yes, but let's go stand on the picnic table anyway.

I can't go on the swing because of a slush puddle.

I can't go down the tube slide because of a slush puddle.
R. Thompson

I can't bounce on the springy duck because of a slush puddle.

All of nature conspires to force me inside to watch TV.
Well, let's go!

mmEEp.
What's that Song?

It's not a Song. It's the note "A."
Mip.
A? A?! I know that letter!
little angel

A is the first letter in ALICE! That's what every-body tells me!
little angel

Hey! DON'T! You'll bend my oboe!
You're playing a song about ME!

I'm just playing the note "A."
"Alice" begins with A, so it's a song about me.
But-
Hey! We should go out in the front yard! You play the song, and I'll dance and wave at traffic!

But-
Come on! You can wear your cape!

Where is everybody? Play louder!
My face hurts. Dance harder!
EEP
R. Thompson

R.Thompson
HEEEE GWEENK OINNG

What are you doing?
Petey's playing the oboe, and I'm dancing and waving at traffic.
HNGEEE

I know how to turn my eyelids inside-out. Can I be in the act, too?
Get your freak show out of here. You're blocking the view.
If he does that eyelid thing, I'm going inside.

Why is your food so far away from each other?
So none of it touches.
I can't digest food if it's touching. I'm pretty sure I have four stomachs, like a cow has.
thompson
Really?
Yeah, one for each food group. It's very rare.
Would you come to my preschool and digest for sharing time?
I'd love to!

Look! what's that?
What?

Oh, it's just a pile of snow.
It's so big.
VAL-U-LESS

They call it Old Mount Soot. It forms in the parking lot every year whether it snows or not.

Mom, can I climb on it?
No, it's dirty.

On its icy, begrimed slopes dwell tiny, dirty trolls called the Sooti. They sneak down and carry off unwary bargain-hunting shoppers to their doom.

Really?
That's why you find abandoned shopping carts everywhere.
R. Thompson

Wow. Nature is so cool.
Look! Here's a cart, and somebody's left all their coupons in it!

Mom says you're the pickiest eater in the world.
Well, I'm not.

The pickiest eater in the world is 108 years old and lives in a cave in France.

Wow, 108! I guess pickiness is a healthy lifestyle.
He eats only bleu cheese and mushrooms. The fungus content must be vital!
R. Thompson

I've discovered I'm the 17th most picky eater in the world.
How do you know?

There's a website I look at on Mom's computer with global pickiness ratings updated hourly.

I could've been 16th, but yesterday I ate a piece of bologna with the rind still on it.
SO CLOSE, PETEY! SO CLOSE!
R. Thompson

OW! Mom.
I'm sorry, Alice.

You have the strangest hair. It's curly on one side, straight on the other, and woolly in back.
Really?

Nature must've intended for me to have three heads, like Petey has four stomachs.
He has what?
Four stomachs, one for each food group.
R. Thompson

Miss Bliss' bun is so big, her hair must be a mile long.
You know what I've heard?
I've heard that the tension required to hold Miss Bliss' hair in place is so great that should her bun suddenly unwind, it'd act as a propellor and lift her way up into the air for hours at a time.

She's got a super-power!
I've heard she uses her power to fight crime, rescue cats from trees and provide drive-time traffic reports!
R. Thompson

My mom was talking about the food pyramid.
We've got a picture of that on our fridge!

On the top is an area for snacks.
On the bottom are things you eat by accident, like dirt, bugs or cough syrup.
R. Thompson

What's in between?
A tasty cream filling, DUH.

Uh-
oh.
Grunt.
GRRRRRR

Oops.
Alice, would you go get Mom, please?
Did your door stick again, Daddy?
I wish my dad's car did tricks.
R. Thompson

C'mon, Petey! You can do it!
Mom, I don't know—

GO, PETEY, GO!
NO, WAIT, I CAAAAAAAA

Omigosh- Petey?
MUSH

PETEY? CAN YOU STAND UP?
I-I don't know-

Yeah, I guess so.

YAY! WHO'S MOM'S BIG BOY? LET'S DO IT AGAIN!
ARE YOU CRAZY? ARE YOU TRYING TO KILL ME?

Is your brother in another awkward stage?
I call it "Keeping Mom's Expectations Low" and I'm all for it.
R. Thompson

I'm learning my first tune! It's called "La-de-Dah."
How's it go?

La-de-Dah, La-de-Dah,

La-de-Dah, La-de-Dah.

It's so beautiful!
Great, now it'll be stuck in my head all day.
R. Thompson

I like your duck!
That's Quackmeyer. He follows me everywhere.

His head's on a spring, so it nods all the time. Whatever I do he's right there, nodding away!
R. Thompson

He's your own personal yes-man!
I know! I'll never have another moment of self-doubt again!

Look what my Mom made for me!
Wow.

It's a charm to repel cooties!
It's an amulet against ear infections.

No, it's a festive juice-box caddy!
Oh.
You'd better wear eye protection when using it.
R. Thompson

Hi, Ms. Otterloop!
Dill! Do you want to see Alice?

No, I'm just checking.
Checking?

Every day I look in everyone's mail slot to check on them, as a community service.
R. Thompson

Boy, look at all the dust bunnies on your stairs!
Bye-bye, Dill.

I hear the cubby on the end is haunted.
Why?

They found a hat in it once with someone's head still inside!
Really? The school brochure doesn't mention a haunted cubby.

You'd think they'd play up an interesting feature like that.
Poor copywriting, I'd say.
R. Thompson

March comes in on clumsy feet,
Kicks the trash cans Down the street,
Knocks the branches Off the Trees,
Gives the power lines a squeeze.

I don't really know how to jump rope.
Doing poetry and sports at the same time is proba-bly dangerous anyway.
R. Thompson

This note says your preschool class is going to the Nature Center!
Is that the place with the dinosaurs?
No, that is the museum.
Is it the place with the giant space aliens?
No, that's the mini-golf course.
Is it the place with that drinking fountain full of sand and old gum?
That's the place!
YUCK. I hate Nature.
R. Thompson

Where are we going again?
The Nature Center! We'll see Ranger Dan!
BLISSHAVEN PRESCHOOL
NATURE CENTER!
WOW.
The Center of Nature!
Ranger Dan mus be real powerfu

bet he ontrols the weather.
I'll bet he ontrols TV.
Can we tell Ranger Dan to put more cartoons on TV?
Children, too much chatter while Miss Bliss is driving makes her very nervous.

Here we are!
CUL DE SAC
NATURE CENTER
R. Thompson

Now please stay together.
Look! There it is!

ALICE.
See? A drinking fountain full of sand and old gum!
Ew.
Yuck.
What kind of gum?

Here are some animals you'd see in the woods!
NATURE CENTER

Ooh! Turtles!
They're not moving.
They look fake.
They are fake.
FAKE!

I'm going to poke my head out and blow their tiny minds!
Nah, it's not worth the effort.
R Thompson

Hi, Ranger Dan!
Ooh, an owl!
Hi, kids! This is Archie! He's got an injured wing.

Owls are smart!
They're so wise!
What happened to him?
He got tangled up in somebody's wind chimes.
R. Thompson

Wind chimes? That's dumb.
You had to tell them.
Hey, they're here to learn.

What did you learn at the Nature Center?
I learned that Dill shouldn't put a pinecone in his mouth.

Oh?
And that Dill shouldn't put an old snakeskin in his mouth.

Oh?
And that nature trails are not made out of trail mix.
R. Thompson

Dill ate some mulch, too?
I learn so many things when I'm with Dill!

Can we go to the toy store?
In a little while.
Daddy, carry me.
Let's walk for now, Alice.

But I'm really, tired! Carry me.
We haven't walked very far.

DADDY, PLEASE? Carry me!
OK, come here. Don't jump.

JUMP
SMACK

GAH-
OOPS.

Can we go to the toy store when Daddy's nose stops bleeding?
Ask him when he comes out of the men's room.
I wish he'd hurry. I'm tired of sitting.
R. Thompson

HEY LOOK! THE MOON IS OUT!
IT'S DAYTIME! THE MOON SHOULDN'T BE OUT!

Something is wrong! The moon snuck into the sky during the day!
No, wait. See, it's because the moo-

What if it's really nighttime?
You mean ...?

Yes! It's nighttime and the sun snuck into the sky!
No!

No wonder I'm tired and cranky! I'm going inside!
Me too!
R. Thompson

But, no, see, the moon goes around the earth... and... um...

I hate being the voice of reason.
Huh?
Alice? Why are you taking a nap?

Don't climb too high on the jungle gym.
Why?

I hear its upper reaches are inhabited by a lost race of wild children with monkey feet and tails.

They subsist on a diet of acorns, squirrels and safety patrol crossing guards.
Acorns? Yuk.
R. Thompson

Look at the kid on this cereal box.

He looks like he's so happy about the cereal that he's lost his mind!

How much of this do I have to eat before I turn into a bug-eyed idiot?

You're right! I'll fix everyone a nice big bowl of oatmeal!
Now see what you've done?
R Thompson

Alice, you are not going out in shorts. It's cold outside!
Dill's outside wearing shorts.

Dill has four older brothers. I think he sometimes gets lost in the mix.
R. thompson

IT'S NOT FAIR!
Well, I'm sorry.

You're not giving me enough cover.
Hey, I'm just one guy.

My duck's spring got stretched. Can you fix it?
I can't. My Dad took my hammer away.

Why?
My Mom said, "A little boy with a hammer? Why not just give him a nail gun, too?"

R. thompson

And...?
That was last month. So far nothing.

Let's sign you up for soccer. Okay, Petey?
Ha, yeah!

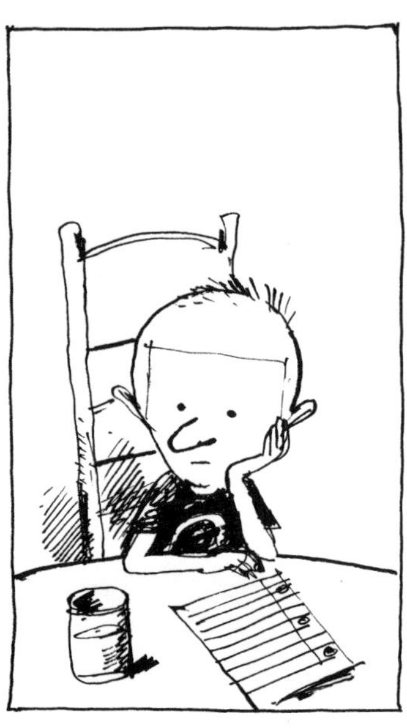

R. Thompson

Did Mom just say something then I said something back?
Then you looked blank. It was a hoot!

I don't want to sign up for soccer.
Oh, Petey! It'll be fun!

No it won't.
Sure, you'll go outside and run around.

But Mom-
Sit on my lap and we'll talk about it...
R. Thompson

Uh-oh, she's got him on her lap. He hasn't got a chance.
Does Petey actually go outside? I'm trying to re-member.

No, don't start counting- HELLO? HELLO? **ALICE?**

You know that job thing Daddy does? I think it makes him grouchy.

Where is he anyway? I made his favorite five-bean salad.

FIVE beans? I separated them into only four piles. Now I have to start all over.

R. Thompson

Where's the trebuchet your brothers built?
It had an accident.
They took it out in a field.

They loaded it up and yanked the cord.
Rthompson

And with a mighty TWANG the whole thing fell apart.
No! What did they load it with?

A bag of marshmallows.
What a senseless waste of good food!
BUPF

Will your brothers build another trebuchet?
Not yet. First I want them to build something for me.
R. Thompson

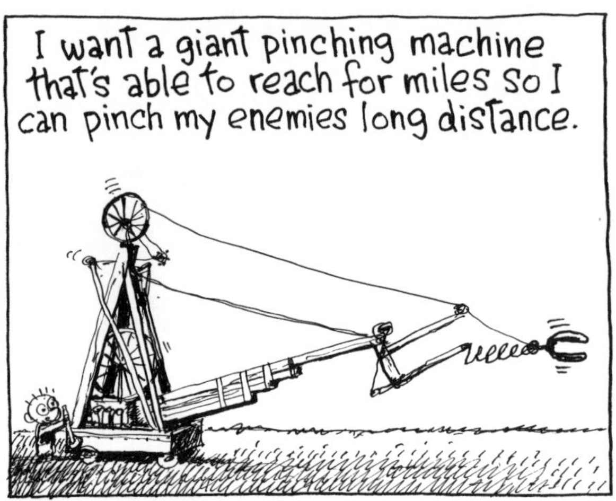
I want a giant pinching machine that's able to reach for miles so I can pinch my enemies long distance.

Dill, you don't have any enemies.
Won't you be glad such a device is in good hands?

So guess what? Miss Bliss is having a contest to name our class!
Uh.
It has to start with a "B."
So we'll be the Blisshaven B-Somethings.
Whoever thinks of the best name gets a prize!
And they get to be Star of the week!

The Blisshaven Brother-Bothering Baloney Brains.
HA! That's way too long!
R. Thompson

We're having a contest to name our class at Blisshaven. It has to start with the "B" sound, whatever that is.

B goes "BUH."
BUH! Buh! Buh buh. Buh buh buh buh buh buh buh buh buh buh buh
R. Thompson

buh buh buh. SPOON! The Blisshaven Spoons!
Butter knife!
Bacteria!
PETEY.

My idea for a class name is The Blisshaven Cows.
That doesn't start with B.

My idea will win because everybody loves cows. They provide us with ice cream and cheese and – what did you say?
"Cow" doesn't start with B.

OK. The Blisshaven Big Bad Brown Cows with Beefy Bottoms. How's that?
Better.
R Sthompson

I didn't win the class-naming contest.
What's the winning name?

The Blisshaven Blooming Blossoms. Nara thought it up.
R. Thompson

That's pretty.
She got a sticker as big as her forehead.

Dill's entry was the Blisshaven Basic Cable Providers!
It was my brother's idea!

Ancient Egyptians were rightly proud of their mummies, which were made by taking one high-ranking dead person, extracting his brains through his nose with a buttonhook, and stuffing him with mayonnaise and garlic, plus some expensive trinkets to impress the other mummies.

It's my turn to use the car now.
No it isn't! I just got in it!

But you've gone off the blacktop onto the dirt.
So?

That means you've gone over the edge of the Earth into a bottomless pit full of alligators and lava, and it's my turn to use the car.

I can't argue with that.
Ha ha ha!
RThompson

Do badgers eat pancakes?
No, they don't.
R. Thompson

GREAT, I spent all day drawing a field guide to nature and it's wrong!

But I think they do like waffles.
Don't be silly. Badgers HATE waffles.

What are you reading?
"Little Neuro." It's my favorite comic.

Little Neuro is a boy who's so frozen with self-consciousness that he never gets out of bed.

Look at him! He's a bulwark of stasis in an active world!

I thought books were about things happening.
Not the ones I read!
R Thompson

Mom and I think you should try soccer.
It's not hard, and it'd be good for you.

You just run around some, kick the ball a few times, and at the end you'll get a little medal and a pizza party.

Pizza with no red sauce?
And the cheese on the side, just the way you like it.

Okay, Petey! Kick the ball right to me!
I'll try, Dad.

KICK

I caught your shoe, Petey!
Hey, the ball didn't move! Do that again, Petey!
R. thompson

That cloud looks like a duck!
All clouds look like ducks.

Yeah! Show us something new!
That one looks like a camel.

Nope, now it looks like a duck, too.
These are the worst clouds ever.
Let's throw mulch at them!
R. Thompson

Alice?

What are you staring at?
I'm wondering what your hair looked like.

Then he said he has hair— it's just scalp-colored.
Sounds like something on a T-shirt you'd give to an old person.

My new soccer shoes are confusing me.
Why?

They're so complicated. They've got all these flanges and flaps and laces and those teeth things on the bottom.

I feel I no longer understand my feet.
Do you want me to yell at them?

Yell at my feet?
I always yell at things I don't understand.
R. Thompson

Mom got me some soccer shoes. I'm not sure if they'll help or not.
Try them with another sport, like paddleball.
Good idea!
R. Thompson

TWANG
TWANG
TWANGK
They didn't help at all.
I thought getting it wrapped around your head was the whole point of paddleball.

What are those things?
Shin guards.

What?
They're to protect your legs from all the other players who are kicking at you.

"Kicking at me"? My whole life is flashing before me.
Who gets to try them out first? Should we line up by size?
R. Thompson

That ball is all flat.
I let most of the air out.
R. Thompson

Why?
It looked all bloated and uncomfortable. I felt sorry for it.

Dill, you're the most thoughtful person I know.
My brother didn't think so when I felt sorry for his bike tires.
PONK

Beni! You've got a new hammer!
No, it's a lint roller.
R. Thompson

How does it work?
You roll it around on clothes.
Ha ha! It tickles!

See all the stuff it picks up?
Ooh! Candy, crayons and army men!
Do it to me! I might have money on me!

I hope the ball doesn't come this way.
If it does, I'll have an out-of-body experience.
R. Thompson

Why?
Because I can see myself failing to kick the ball.

Oh, yeah.
You need to be more supportive of yourself.
Huh?

Yeah!
Huh?
What?
You need a cheering section!

YEAH! YEAH!
YAY!
PETEY, PETEY, HE'S OUR GUY! IF HE CAN'T DO IT, I DON'T KNOW—

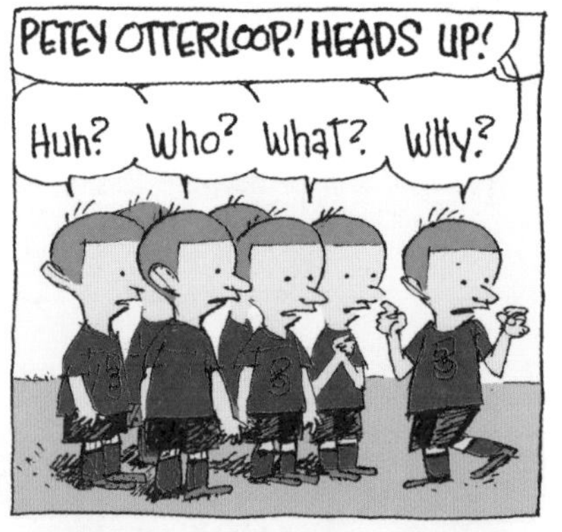
PETEY OTTERLOOP! HEADS UP!
Huh?
Who?
What?
Why?

WHAM

Mom, was that a strike?
Was it? Shoot, I missed it.

Beni! You did get a new hammer!
My mom gave it to me. Watch what it does.

SKWEEK
SKWEEK
SKWEEK
SKWEEK

SKWEEK
SKWEEK
SKWEEK
SKWIK
R Thompson

Is it a clown hammer?
Who wants to fix clowns?
Well, not as a career.

Look, Petey! It's your new soccer shirt!
It's so red. HEY! My name is spelled wrong!
PEVEY! OH, NO-
PEVEY
Nobody is named "PEVEY."

Well-

It can be your secret soccer player identity. You'll be BIG RED PEVEY!
That'd strike fear into the opposing team, right?
PEVEY
R. Thompson

Look, Alice, it's my new soccer shirt!
It's so red.
Only my name is spelled "Pevey."
Red makes bulls mad.
So now I'm Big Red-huh, what?
Bulls get mad and they run over you.

MOM! ARE THERE BULLS ON THE SOCCER FIELD?
I saw that on an old TV cartoon!
Me too! And the goat ate all the tin cans!
R. Thompson

That cloud looks like a TV set.
That one looks like a computer monitor.

That one looks like a monkey with a banjo.
Where?

There. Oops, now his head is drifting away.
I don't see–

Now it's growing a new head. And the banjo's turned into a club.
Where? Where?

It's got a dragon head! And tentacles! And look! Great big bat wings!
I still don't–

SEE? FLAMES BILLOW FROM ITS JAWS AS IT DESCENDS IN AWFUL MAJESTY!
NO! AAAGH.

R. Thompson 4/13

Now it looks like a guy eating soup.
Oh, thank God.